A Year at the Races

Text by

ROBERT B.
PARKER
&
JOAN H.
PARKER

Photographs by

WILLIAM
STRODE

Design by Amy Hill

VIKING

A Year at the RACES

VIKING
Published by the Penguin Group
Viking Penguin, a division of Penguin Books USA Inc.,
375 Hudson Street, New York, New York 10014, U.S.A.
Penguin Books Ltd, 27 Wrights Lane,
London W8 5TZ, England
Penguin Books Australia Ltd, Ringwood,
Victoria, Australia
Penguin Books Canada Ltd, 2801 John Street,
Markham, Ontario, Canada L3R 1B4
Penguin Books (N.Z.) Ltd, 182-190 Wairau Road,
Auckland 10, New Zealand

Penguin Books Ltd, Registered Offices:
Harmondsworth, Middlesex, England

First published in 1990 by Viking Penguin,
a division of Penguin Books USA Inc.

10 9 8 7 6 5 4 3 2

Text copyright © Robert B. Parker and Joan H. Parker, 1990
Photographs copyright © William Strode, 1990
All rights reserved

LIBRARY OF CONGRESS CATALOGING IN PUBLICATION DATA
Parker, Robert B., 1932–
A year at the races/text by Robert B. Parker & Joan H. Parker;
photographs by William Strode.
p. cm.
ISBN 0 670 82678 2
1. Horse-racing. 2. Horse-racing–United States. I. Parker,
Joan H. II. Strode, William. III. Title.
[SF335.5P37 1990]
799.4′00973–dc20   89-40797

Printed in Japan
Set in Cloister and Liberty

This is for Helen Brann

A bad day at the races is better than a good day anywhere else.

Acknowledgments

For their unstinting help and generosity, their hospitality and humor, their expertise, our deepest gratitude goes to Anne and Cot Campbell.

We thank Bill Strode for his excellent eye, and his camaraderie in an assortment of places all over the country.

For all kinds of time and effort, our thanks are due to the staff at Dogwood Stable and in particular to the indefatigable Lawson Glenn.

The trainers, among them Neil Howard and Charlie Fenwick, were informative and invaluable; along with Ron Stevens at Aiken, South Carolina, who shared with us the experience of starting very young horses on their training program.

We were welcomed at Claiborne Farm by one of the grooms, who gave us a terrific tour and allowed us to pat the great Secretariat on the nose.

Thanks to all the people at the tracks we visited, at Saratoga, Keeneland, Hialeah, Gulfstream, and Fair Hills; the young women exercise riders; the grooms, particularly Willie Woods; and all the people tending the shedrows.

We found the horse museums at Saratoga and Lexington a source of much valuable information presented brilliantly.

Our deep appreciation to our editor, Amanda Vaill, whose love for horses and Thoroughbred racing has shone through her work on this book.

Contents

A Year at the Races

PREFACE

I know nothing of racing. I had been to a race only once, in 1958, when I went to Rockingham Park in New Hampshire with a guy named Dick Bartlett and we came out about thirty dollars ahead, having just missed a long shot in the last race. With our winnings we took my wife out to dinner in Lawrence, Mass. And blew the thirty, which was about what dinner for three cost in Lawrence, Mass., in 1958 when we were not yet twenty-six and life's flower had barely begun to bud.

I know nothing of horses. The last time I was astride one, a riding stable nag on top of a mountain in the state of Washington, one of its stable mates kicked me in the shin, causing a hematoma the size of the Gadsden Purchase and the color of an eggplant.

Joan knows much less about these things than I do. Though much more about everything else. Thus when we came to this book we were a *tabula rasa*, and the next year's travels would have plenty of room to write upon us.

What we learned in a year of hanging around the Dogwood Stable operation is chronicled in the music of Bill Strode's pictures, and in our few modest lyrics. Clearly we have gleaned when others, more informed, might have reaped richly. But there was in our innocence the possibility that an emperor would stroll by, and we would see that he had no clothes. I don't think we quite saw a naked emperor, but there were some things that struck as we strolled about racetracks and shedrows that are hard to categorize but which, it seems to me, deserve to be said.

The central fact of thoroughbred racing, to us rank outsiders, seems to be money. Horses are judged on how much they've won. This is not simply greed (though it's not charity either); it is, rather, as in so many branches of human pursuit (including ours), the way they keep score. People bet on thoroughbred racing. It's what distinguishes it from horse shows.

ABOVE: What it's all about: Champion Personal Ensign comes back to the winner's circle at Churchill Downs after a victory in the Breeder's Cup.

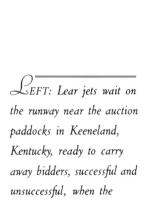

LEFT: Lear jets wait on the runway near the auction paddocks in Keeneland, Kentucky, ready to carry away bidders, successful and unsuccessful, when the yearling sales are over.

While no one gets into the horse business, I think, without liking horses (it's a hard go; if you didn't like horses you might as well be a broker), horse people remember that these horses are for sale. They are not pets. Thoroughbreds are functionary. People who own dogs, even pointer bitches that, perhaps occasionally, in midwinter, or in midsummer when the air conditioning is on, or in fall or spring when the windows are open, now and then slip under the covers in bed with you, don't quite get it about people who deal in thoroughbreds.

In the breeding shed at Claiborne Farm, one of the foremost Thoroughbred breeding farms, the walls are padded. When it is in use there are several grooms handy to make sure that neither stallion nor mare is damaged in the process. Even conception is a managed process. Humans have their hand on a thoroughbred at every significant juncture of its life. Thoroughbreds have little to do with the image of wild horses running free.

Morning at the barn: a horse is returned to his stall after exercise.

The image is only that. Practically all the wild horses on earth are feral. Only an occasional Onager in central Asia somewhere descends unbroken from a wild ancestry.

Horses are herd animals, but thoroughbreds are too valuable to be allowed to herd. They tend to fight sometimes, the stallions especially. And when you've invested $750,000 in a gray colt whose grandfather was Seattle Slew, you don't want one of your old studs kicking hell out of him to keep him away from the mares.

Thoroughbreds are an anomaly, a human creation of narrow purpose and very specific design. They are magnificent. The word is greatly overused when talking of racehorses, but it is truly appropriate for these animals who are seemly in proportion and as comely as any animal alive (except perhaps female pointers). Yet they are as fragile as crystal stemware. On the one hand, breeding continues to create ever-increasing aerobic capacities; on the other hand, breeding continues to produce horses with lighter and lighter skeletal frames, frames less and less able to support the speed that the heart-lung evolution has made possible. The tension between bone mass and lung capacity never eases.

What is at work in the world of thoroughbred racing

is, I think, simply hope. Every spring there are new yearlings. Every year one might turn out to be Secretariat, or Ruffian. Every year starts over at the auctions. The people who work in the racing business say they like horses. They say they like the life, the pageantry, the membership in a specialized fan club, the sport of kings. But you cannot be around racing very much without hearing somebody say that no one ever committed suicide with an untried two-year-old in the barn. That's what they love—not horses, not pageantry, not even the money. What they pursue is possibility. They love hope. And because they do, they are very good to be around.

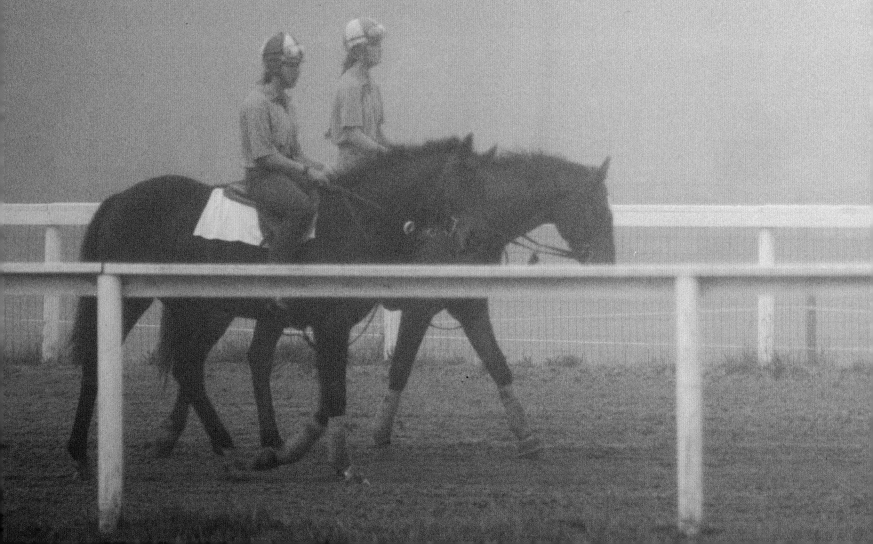

HORSES IN

THE MORNING

ABOVE: An exercise rider's grin lights up the early morning darkness.

Racehorses get up early as hell. I have never been able to discover if that's because they like it, or the grooms like it, or the owners like it. What I know for sure is that I don't like it much, and Joan, whose preparations to face the day are more convolute than mine (and produce infinitely better results), considers it barbaric.

But there we were, backside, Saratoga, at six in the morning, looking at horses. Most of them have already been out on the track in front of the empty grandstands, running around the silent infield, the exercise riders in jeans and T-shirts, whips stuck in boot tops or wedged in belts at the small of their back. They are small by

*W*hen the horses come out of the barn in the morning, it's still early enough for the grass to be wet.

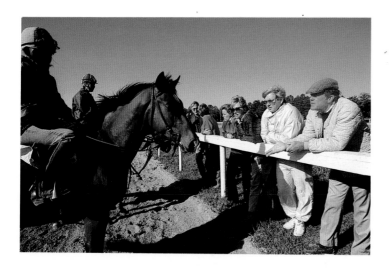

street standards but generally too big to be jockeys. Many
of them are women. They manage the half-ton overbred
animals in the still morning the way a kid rides a bicycle.
They talk among themselves as they ride, but we're too
far, standing slightly elevated, watching, to hear them.
What we hear is the patterned chuff of the horses' hooves
muffled by the deep soft surface of the track, and the
harsh snorting billows of the horses breathing as they
are let out into the sprinting run called breezing. Joan
watches as she does, absorbed with what goes on before
her. A city kid, I am sniffing the air for coffee. Joan is
a city kid too, but she adjusts — even to watching horses
at six A.M.

It is as if we have stepped into an old stereopticon,
a vision of America when Currier and Ives were chil-

dren. The horses in the green morning, still cool enough for the grass to be wet, the desultory conversations, unvarying through the eternity of green mornings, as the horses circle the placid track, counterclockwise. We hear only the animals. There are cars parked along the backstretch, and trucks, and if you listen hard you can probably hear a radio from the shedrow area playing a golden oldie by Pink Floyd. But the cars and the trucks and Pink

A few backstretch spectators watch a young horse, accompanied by an outrider on a pony, go for a morning gallop.

Morning mist shrouds two horses, one (R.) a Thoroughbred ready for a workout, the other the trainer's pony, as they stand out on the training track.

Floyd are insubstantial, evanescent in the eternal green morning, where reality radiates from the horses in their stately rush around the otherwise empty track.

It is conventional to say they are beautiful. Someone always says it. But how beautiful they are is a little startling. Most of them look alike. They ought to; they all descend from one of three stallions, the majority from one, called the Darley Arabian. They are brown, mostly, ranging to reddish chestnut at one end of the spectrum to a blackish bay at the other. Occasionally one sees a gray, usual-

ly with a roan dappling, and occasionally a red roan. I am told there are blacks, but I haven't seen any. Nor have I seen any whites. Mounted and saddled, they look less beautiful to my innocent, city-bred eye. With a rider up, they seem more a means of conveyance, an artifact designed by selective breeding and sophisticated training to transport a man from start to finish. They are bred for this, we are told; they love to run. And it is clear that many of the horses are being held in as they exercise, necks bowed, prancing and trying to toss their heads. But we have also noticed that when they succeed in throwing their rider, they head for the barn. People say many things about what horses think and feel; but the horses seem to know things that they aren't revealing.

When a Thoroughbred breezes through the stretch in the morning, all you hear is the pounding of hooves.

37

After a morning workout, a bath. Sometimes the groom will just turn the hose on the horse; other times a bucket and sponge do the job.

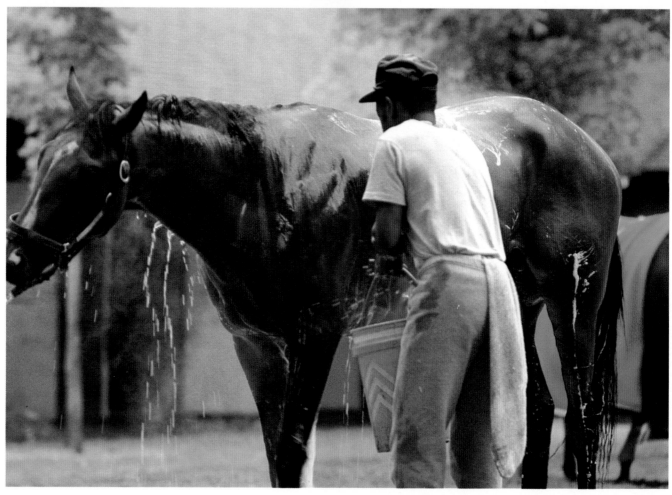

The horse's cooler, a light muslin or mesh blanket that performs the same function as an athlete's warm-up suit, looks like a diaphanous bathrobe.

I like them best now, in the stableyard, unsaddled, standing with that enigmatic stare. Now we are at the Dogwood Stable barn, looking at Dogwood horses being washed. They are lathered from big buckets and scrubbed one at a time by a groom, a young woman in jeans and a green Dogwood T-shirt, her blond hair cut short. She has high-top Reeboks on her feet, half laced, the cuffless bottom of her jeans caught behind the tongue of the shoe. The horse lowers his head a bit and stands that way, gazing with his big, passionless eyes, turning his head around the way horses do, now and then, to see what's happening. She scrubs and lathers and sluices him off with a hose. There is no nozzle on the hose; she controls the flow with her thumb, the way a kid does washing his car in the driveway on a summer afternoon, with the ball game playing meaninglessly on the screen porch. The translucent rope of silvery water glasses out over the surface of the horse and sluices the suds away, and the horse shines in the morning light. A hint of steam rises off his flanks. All down the center aisle of the stable row, the horses are being washed clean. Some of them are draped in a kind of white bathrobe, made diaphanous by the sun shining through it, outlining the horses' legs the way it sometimes happens with good-looking women in summer dresses. This is when they are beautiful, here, dismounted, silent, standing still, a thousand pounds of muscle and bone and lung capacity carried on legs as graceful as an antelope's, with ankles smaller than mine.

After chores are done and the horses put away, it's time to sit down for a few minutes with the Racing Form.

There are some who wish to kill you, whose implacable and single-minded goal seems to be your death. Some of these are handled like cobras, two grooms to lead them out while the rider is up, two outriders, one on either side. They get special harness, their stalls are closed or screened to keep them from reaching out and taking a finger as you stroll by on your way to feed the next horse down. But mostly, especially here, after they have been run on the track and hot-walked and washed, they are as tranquil as mountain lakes: still, beautiful, calm, and inward, submitting elegantly to the bathing and the brushing, and to being kissed on the nose by a blond groom in Dogwood green and Reeboks.

Washed and dried, they are put in their stalls, where they stand looking out, their heads over the half door, taking it in, looking like those old pictures of French prostitutes in Montmartre, gazing out of the windows of their rooms, luring the farm boys under the gaslights.

By eight o'clock the backstretch morning is over. It is time for breakfast. It has, for me, in fact, been time for breakfast for something more than three hours, but it turns out to have been worth the wait. Cot Campbell has invited us to breakfast at The Reading Room. The Reading Room is a Victorian house with a wide veranda, adjacent to the track at Saratoga. It is, I understand, for members only, but I never did know of what one must be a member. I wasn't a member of anything. The last organization I belonged to sent me to Korea, and I've never belonged to anything since.

We sit on the wide veranda behind an exclusive box hedge seven feet high and are served fresh orange juice and coffee by a young man in a white coat. We order the local specialty, hand melon, which tastes suspiciously like cantaloupe, and hotcakes. I feel as if Fort Sumter

Workout over, this horse watches the scene from his stall door.

The Reading Room is actually a whole house, a white Victorian adjacent to the Saratoga track.

42

is about to be fired on. Joan, who but moments ago had looked exactly right for visiting the backstretch at six A.M., now looks exactly appropriate to an elegant veranda breakfast with bone china and a waiter in a white coat. I still look appropriate to the backstretch, but no one seems to mind. Joan suggests that perhaps I always look appropriate to the backstretch.

Cot Campbell looks a bit like Henry Fonda, the kind of guy who can wear a soft snap-brim hat tipped way forward over the bridge of his nose and still look like Henry Fonda. When I do it I look like Wallace Beery. Who was also, I suppose, appropriate to the backstretch. Cot is the president, CEO, founder, and heartbeat of Dogwood Stable. He is not a breeder. He buys yearlings and syndicates them. Since about six thoroughbreds in a hundred ever win a stakes race, and since the purchase and training and care and feeding of yearling thoroughbreds demands an enormous capital outlay, a man who does what Cot does needs the *cojones* of a cat burglar. He's got one of those shuffling-through-the-meadow-chewing-on-a-sprout-of-new-cut-grass Georgia drawls; but no one is confused. His wife, Anne, is with him, as she almost always is. She is lovely, Southern, funny, stable,

and charming. I would buy a horse from her anytime she asked.

Some Dogwood owners are with us. They have bought shares in some of Cot's horses. If the horses all look the same to me, it's because I'm not an owner. These people know the horses, the times, the purses. They know jockeys and trainers. Do they like horses? They say they do, but I'm not certain. I think maybe what they like is racing.

There's a difference.

Would I like to buy in? Cot is not a pushy guy, but there's all that overhead, and here I am, and the conversation has swung around in that direction.

Joan suggests that if I owned a horse, I would be feeding it horsie treats and teaching it to give me a wet kiss on the nose.

"He has a female pointer," Joan says, "that sleeps in the bed, under the covers."

There is silence for a moment at the table. Then the conversation moves on. No one returns to the question of my purchasing a horse. The kid in the white coat pours more coffee into my bone china cup. I look at Joan with the summer sun shining on her hair. I sip a little coffee. I feel like Cornelius Vanderbilt.

AUCTION

*S*ome racing stables breed horses. *Secretariat is at stud, for instance, at Claiborne Farms in Lexington; and when he's not working, you* can stop by and visit him. Some racing stables are only in the game for the racing; when a horse retires, he's sold, and when they need a new horse, they have to buy him. A very few outfits, like Dogwood, buy horses and train them and race them and sell shares in them to people who like horses or racing or both. And these investors, as is true of many in the racing world, prefer horses that are going to win. Thus the matter of purchasing a yearling is the first in a series of hair-raising decisions that help Cot Campbell stay lean and alert.

In the shedrows the horses wait, on display. Handlers bring them out, combed, curried, and gleaming. Cot and Ron Stevens, the trainer, look at some of them. They look at the legs, the neck, the legs, the withers, the legs. They check the teeth, feel the legs, stand back to watch the gait, get close to run a hand on the legs. No one seems to fear a kick in the head during all this. Well, almost no one. I am careful to keep Joan between me and the horses as we watch.

Lore abounds in the sales paddocks as the buyers move among the horses, each clutching the auction catalogue, full of whose dam won what and who had sired whom. It reads like the begat section in Genesis. Beware horses with white stockings, because the hooves will chip (though Secretariat has white stockings). Avoid cribbers (horses who chew on wood) or weavers (horses that sway head and neck ceaselessly, the way caged lions pace). Gait analysis properly applied will tell you which is a great horse. Breeding, carefully evaluated, will tell you which is a great horse. Intuition will tell you. God will tell you. Maybe I will.

Buying a yearling is a science as inexact as picking a winner. Seattle Slew could not pass the admissions test

Cot Campbell marks comments about the yearlings in the sales catalogue.

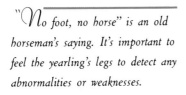

Is this the one? This yearling gets careful scrutiny.

"No foot, no horse" is an old horseman's saying. It's important to feel the yearling's legs to detect any abnormalities or weaknesses.

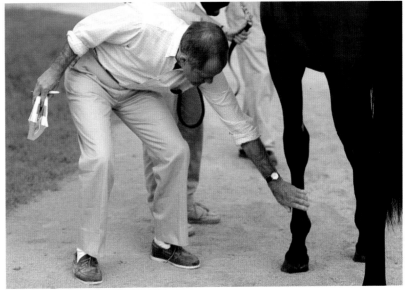

to the Keeneland Select Auction. He was sold for $17,500 at a minor yearling sale in 1975. In 1977 he won the Triple Crown. His stud fees are forty times his purchase price—per, ah, shot. John Henry went for $1,100. He ended up winning $6,597,947. Everyone is looking for horses like these. Everyone was looking for them then. Horse people say, finally, what makes a great horse is heart, the willingness to dig down and drag it up and drive its own magnificent machinery harder and longer

Business as usual in the shady sales paddocks combines serious consideration with shared memories and jokes.

than the horses it's running against. At one year, there's no way to test for heart, so you try to cover everything else, and hope.... Better look at those legs again.

In the August evening, the auction amphitheater is full. Groundlings hover outside, looking in through the half-misted windows, where the hot night interacts with the interior air conditioning. There are television control trailers hauled up outside and the cable lash tops running in. People are dressed for the evening. Most wear ties and jackets. Some wear evening dress. Some wear blue jeans and Ban-lon T-shirts. In the center of the amphitheater there is a high auctioneer's pulpit, and before it, a low stage carpeted with some sort of mulch. The horses come down a ramp from the holding area, led

"Let me hear two, two hundred thousand, will ya?" chants auctioneer Ralph Retler as the spotter looks for a bid from the audience.

The spotter has a bid.

by a groom. They are nervous, tossing their heads, showing a lot of eyeball. Many demonstrate, in their anxiety, the wisdom of carpeting the stage with mulch. A groom with a shovel stands by.

The auctioneers are tuxedoed, flawless, poised, and amused. There are spotters everywhere; no bids are overlooked. I suspect an occasional phantom bid, but I'm a cynical city kid, and surely I am wrong. Horses are bought for $15,000, for $235,000, a million, a million two. The one that went for $15,000 looks better than the one that went for a million two. Or at least I think so. Joan thinks so too.

"It appears," I murmur thoughtfully, "that beauty is only skin deep."

"It does," Joan says. She smiles. There is a hint of resignation in her smile.

A ripple of excitement undulates through the crowd. *The Arabs* have arrived. The prices will really soar. Inside the arena, the air conditioning labors in semi-vain. It's cooler inside than out. But it is not cool. I am wearing tie and jacket. I am not comfortable. All the men are wearing ties and jackets. None have removed them. I wait for an intensely contested surge in the bidding, and when everyone's attention is focused on a dark bay or brown colt, I loosen my tie. The colt goes to *the Arabs* for $2.5 million. Everyone turns and stares at *the Arabs*. I do too, but I never see any.

"You see any Arabs?" I whisper to Joan.

"I think they're in disguise," Joan whispers back. "Coats and ties."

"Of course."

Another stir rustles through the crowd. Heads turn toward the center aisle. A woman comes down the aisle, fashionably late, making an entrance, all in white.

"Is it Little Bo Peep?" Joan whispers.

"She doesn't have a crook," I whisper back.

"Good point," Joan says.

The bid board shows $4,600,00 for the horse in the ring; auctioneer Retler and master of ceremonies John Finney, in the raised stand in the foreground, look as if they're asking for more.

We are told that it is, indeed, not Little Bo Peep but a famous racing and society person, the kind that comes from two places: of Palm Beach and Saratoga, or East Hampton and Old Lyme, or some such.

"I was from two places when I was in the army in Korea," I said.

"Of Boston and Yongdungp'o?" Joan thinks a minute. "I don't think that counts."

Late in the evening, Cot buys a bay colt. His goal, as is almost everyone's, is not simply to buy the best horse but to buy the best horse for the money. His bid does not threaten the evening's record set by *the Arabs*, but it is a large sum, and all of us look at this nervous, head-tossing, eye-rolling year-old male horse that stands at the end of the short shank the groom holds, jiggling it occasionally to reassure the horse, help him to show well. All of us think the same thing. Will he run? Will he get himself in on the rail half a length behind, going down the stretch, and elongate that stride and drive himself, with his lungs sucking air and his heart near bursting and his neck thrust on out toward the finish line and everything now a blur of sound and motion—will he burst past that horse on his right shoulder and get his nose under the

Cot Campbell ponders a bid . . .

58

wire first not because the jockey urges him but because it is what he was created for? That's what no one can ever know, looking at a one-year-old male horse that you just paid a ton for.

Will he run? He might.

Payment is due on the spot; letters of credit have been arranged. Bank checks are accepted, traveler's checks. Shipping instructions are made, the auction runs on, but we have done our business, and we leave, out into the thick upstate night, through the outside onlookers peering through the foggy windows, heading for the parking lot.

"What happens," I speculate, "if when the new horse is being loaded into the truck he stumbles and breaks his right foreleg?"

Everyone gazes at me with a pained expression.

"This is a scary business," Joan says.

Yes.

. . . then seems to be afraid to look at the board.

The steeplechase is a long race. It requires barriers and hurdles and enough room to build a shopping center. Which is why the Breeder's Cup Steeplechase was held somewhere west of Sirius the Dog Star, in Fair Hill, Maryland. If you live in Boston and you wish to go there, you fly to New York and get into a limo your companions have arranged and drive for longer than our honeymoon lasted down the Jersey Pike. Our driver was a New Yorker, a man who knew the city the way your tongue knows the contours of your teeth. Unfortunately we weren't in the city. We spent much of our time lost in New Jersey (which sounds like the title of an apocalyptic play). For a considerable

The saddling area at the steeplechase racecourse at Fair Hill. The atmosphere is more that of a country fair than a racetrack.

LEFT: Weighing out (which occurs before the race—you weigh in when you return from the track) at Fair Hill. Steeplechase horses carry from twenty to thirty pounds more than their flat-racing counterparts, and all of it over jumps, frequently for distances of more than two miles.

period he was driving us to Laurel Racecourse, near Baltimore. When we dissuaded him from this and pointed him toward Fair Hill, we spent even more time lost in Maryland, until the passengers mutinied and took over the car, and we got to the track. We would have mutinied earlier, but we were distracted by the very large picnic lunch that Helen Brann had packed.

Fair Hill Steeplechase looks like nothing so much as a country fairground. It is rural, and rolling, and thronged with people in furs and bib overalls. Joan was first out of the car.

"One small step for a man," she said. "One giant leap for mankind."

There were many food stalls where sausages were frying. I gazed at the one closest. Onions and peppers were frying with the sausage. Beer was available.

"Wholesome country fare," I said to Joan.

"You already ate a whole chicken," Joan said.

"Not the bones," I said.

"Yes," she said. "I was proud of that."

I had come down to Maryland to see one of Dogwood's horses, a big, dark colt named Kesslin, run. I was there with the women who manage my life: Helen Brann, who

$\mathcal{R}$acegoer at Fair Hill.

$\mathcal{A}$fter saddling up (TOP RIGHT) there's time to chat in the Fair Hill box area.

is my literary agent; Flora Roberts, who is my dramatic-rights agent; and Joan Parker, who is the source of music from beyond a distant hill. We joined the Campbells in their reserve box. At Fair Hill, reserve boxes are sectioned off with pipe railing and supplied with folding chairs, like the ones used in bingo parlors and in the cellars of churches where bean suppers are served with thin slices of canned ham.

In front of us, the steeplechase course rolls away, scattered with hazards, up a far hill. Copses of trees stand about. There are some rural-looking buildings in the middle distance, and the long serpentine of the course fence trailing across. It is like an English print: a race being held in a meadow, the riders' silks bright and almost intrusive in the placid landscape.

There is a lot of excitement. Kesslin has finished strong in his last several races. He is expected to win today, and we are all there to watch him do it. He is a handsome animal. He looks like he should win. Like most steeplechasers, he's big and rangy, almost black, in a color the auction catalogues insist on calling "dark bay or brown," and the muscular arch of his neck and the almost sumptuous roll of his haunches as he walks speak of power and heart.

Kesslin looks ready to run.

He gallops down to the start.

The chicken is wearing off. Between the third and fourth races, I go and purchase box lunches for us, proudly eschewing the sausages with fried peppers that perfume the air behind the stands, rich with the promise of coronary occlusion. The sandwiches are good. Actual sandwiches, made in someone's kitchen and wrapped in wax paper and delivered in a cardboard box to the church booth where they are sold to benefit a youth group.

Cot and Anne are quiet as Kesslin and the other horses head out to the top of the far hill toward the start. They

are very small when they start, very far away. Too far away to hear hoofbeats. Rather we watch them in silence. They move without sound down the long, easy slope at the start of the course. Cot has his glasses on them; Anne does too. It's a long race. The crowd watches quietly. There is none of the frenzy of a flat race, once around the oval, where the audience is reaching out almost physically, dragging their horse forward, achingly, strained, compelled, trying to will the animal one yard faster, one

. . . and over the first fence.

Cot and Anne Campbell watch the race.

One of the jockeys—not Kesslin's—falls, but he is unhurt.

foot, one inch. Here the soundlessness of the horses' progress is matched by the quietude of the crowd. It will yell, and pray, and strain its soul toward the horse of its choice later, but now it is at peace as the horses move in their panoramic stillness, like the figures in a pageant across the grassy hillside.

It is probably how racing once was, and I think as I watch how maybe it's the way it still should be: rural, spacious, leisurely.

Kesslin is running easily in third as they come onto the level ground. He is where they want him to be as he swings around the course and past us in the grandstand. And now we can hear them, the hooves thumping

CHAMPAGNE

against the grass racecourse, the breath blowing out and rushing in. He takes the hurdles easily. They swing out wide again, receding from us, the sound dying, as they make their last loop of the course. Next time past, it will be for everything, and the sound of the horses will be drowned by the sound of the stands.

Cot has the glasses fixed to his eyes. Without them it is hard to make much sense out of the blurring line of silks crouched over the big animals.

The horses are over the last fence, and into the stretch.

"How's he running?" someone asks.

"Strong," Cot says. His voice is quiet. He doesn't show the strain except for the quietness, the inwardness, as he focuses all of himself on the horse running along the far turn of the course.

"Still in third?"

"Yeah. It's what we planned—he'll ask him the question at the last turn."

And then they are at the last turn and coming down the stretch toward us, and the sound in the stands rises as they come. I cannot make them out. They look like a sea of horses, heads and necks and shoulders, the silks of the jockeys above them, riding the crest of this wave of pounding horseflesh. I look for the Dogwood green and yellow, and see it, and lose it and see it again, and then it is gone and then they are close upon us and then they are past us and Kesslin isn't there. Cot has seen it already and is out of the stands and out on the track.

"Where the hell is Kesslin?"

"Pulled up," Anne says, "just at the top of the stretch."

"Hurt?"

"I don't know."

I see him now, far down the track. The jockey off, hold-

Something has happened to Kesslin: Cot and Anne Campbell try to find him through their bincoculars.

Cot goes out on the track to find out what went wrong. It's not a good way to end the day.

ing Kesslin's reins, the two of them walking slowly in; and Cot in a plaid jacket, the glasses now slung over his shoulder, walking alone down the course toward them. The stands are buzzing about the winners; our booth is silent as we watch Cot walk toward his horse. The track is made to horse scale. A man looks out of place there on foot, very small.

Anne is too graceful to show tension. But it is there, in back of her eyes a little, in the way she keeps watching them, the two men and the horse as they walk in together.

Kesslin is led off the track. Cot comes back to our box.

He looks for Anne as he comes. Their eyes meet. He nods a little, and smiles. Cot is not a man for large gestures.

"I think it's all right," Anne says.

And it is.

"The boy pulled him up," Cot says. "Said the horse may have pulled a muscle on the last jump, and he didn't want to take a chance with him. But I don't think it's serious."

"The rider did the right thing," someone says.

"Yes," Cot says. "There are other races."

All's well that ends well, though: Kesslin will race another day.

AIKEN

It's morning along the shedrow: eyes fixed on an approaching visitor, this horse is hoping for his breakfast.

To reach Aiken, South Carolina, you fly to Atlanta, trek through Atlanta Airport, rent a car, and drive southeast through the red-clay Georgia countryside past Augusta, across the Savannah River, and into South Carolina. You take a right off Route 20 and drive through overarching trees into Aiken. Unless you're a horse.

If you're a horse you come overland by commodious trailer, hauled by people whose business is hauling horses. It takes longer, but you avoid Atlanta Airport.

Aiken is the headquarters of Dogwood Stable, and there is a training track at Aiken where the year-old horses that have been trucked in from the auction sites learn

to be racehorses. Some learn to be better racehorses than others; but that is what makes horse races. If you walk to the training track, you come through a corridor of tall Southern pines, branchless as ship masts for fifty feet before the top branches umbrella out and shade the corridor below. It is a dirt road, and the sifting fall of needles for sixty or seventy years has hushed the tree floor on both sides, so that there is a kind of acoustic solemnity that pervades the road. At the far end, narrowed to the length of a single horse by perspective, you can see the track, unshaded, a brightening across which a horse and rider move in silhouette; seeming, framed as they are in the sudden light, almost volitionless; too far away to hear the creak of harness or the huff of the horse's breath, there is only that soft chuff of the hooves in the track, a sound not available in the macadamized world, a sound that belongs here, in the permanent nineteenth

A young horse jogs around the training track.

Fresh wood shavings are put into each horse's stall in the morning, and the old bedding is shoveled away.

century, in the world of horses and riders and colonnaded dirt roads, where late fall is as warm as summer and the rider and horse seem blended by perspective into a single centaur. For a moment they are there, and then, effortlessly, they are gone.

OPPOSITE: Rider Julie Stewart carries a saddle and bridle from the tack room to her horse's stall.

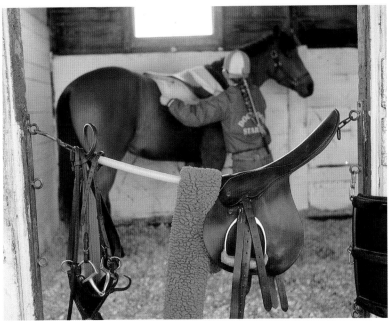

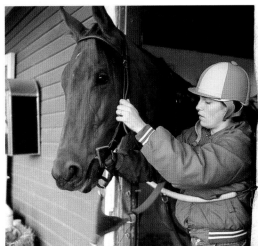

It is November, and the babies that Cot Campbell bought at Saratoga and Keeneland are being introduced to the sport of kings. Joan and I are at the circular training ring, where a big-eyed chestnut filly is being introduced first to the saddle and later to a rider. A groom holds the lead while the rider shows the saddle to the filly and then puts it against her and then finally puts it on. The filly tosses her head a little and blows through her nose, but is generally easy about it.

At trainer Ron Stevens's weekly barn meeting, the stable staff is kept up to date on each horse's progress and regimen.

The kind of horse-breaking one sees in western movies and beer commercials is foreign to this operation. Dogwood Stable is not a rodeo. By gentle increments, the horse gets used to the saddle and bridle, until it strolls around the training ring, on a long lead, saddled and bridled. Then the rider, a young woman with a very long single braid, lies across the saddle for a bit, and finally rides the filly, upright, feet in the stirrups. The filly walks, a little peckish but steady, around the training ring like a grown-up girl.

A yearling becomes accustomed to the idea of weight on his back: Diana Bosco lies across the saddle while he's led around the saddling ring. Only later will Diane sit upright, feet in the stirrups.

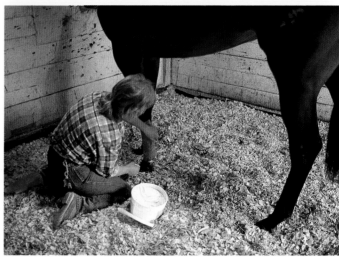

OPPOSITE: *Workout done, horses and grooms have time for a few minutes in the sun.* BELOW: *Padded bandages protect the horses' legs from knocks and scrapes.*

Is the cat company for the horse, or vice versa?

90

Dogwood at the training track is a tight ship. The stable crew, mostly young, frequently female, are neat in green T-shirts and often-washed jeans. The stable area is as well groomed as a golf course. The stalls are clean, the horses are clean. Walking about in my casual attire, I feel as if I'm littering. There are a few stable cats, but there are no dogs allowed around the stables. The ban does not cover Ron Stevens's dog, a colliesque animal that sleeps in lordly exception in the barn office. In addition to the yearlings there are other horses. There's a four-year-old named Orfano, whose dam died at his birth. He's been purchased in England and is being readied for the American track. There is Russian Affair, the venomous three-year-old we saw at Saratoga. He wears the same inward, enigmatic expression all the horses wear. There's no way to tell he's dangerous, except that if you come near him he tries to kill you. One of the many things that I found fascinating in the world of horse racing was the ease with which a 115-pound teenage girl can manage a half-ton horse. Even the mean one is handled carefully, but by no means gingerly, by kids a tenth his size.

In a rare moment of relaxation, Julie Stewart reads her mail.

*R*IGHT: The babies stand quietly in the starting gate, just getting used to it. BELOW: Later, they will gallop in pairs.

The stallions, of course, can be the most difficult, and in extreme cases gelding can have a calming effect. But its effect on stud fees is deleterious, and gelding is avoided if possible. No one wants to geld a two-year-old that turns out to be John Henry. No one wants to end a bloodline that traces back to the Byerly Turk.

At the appropriate moment in their training, when they are used to being ridden, the babies are introduced to the starting gate. On a lovely November morning, Joan and I are there to watch as four of them come at a slow walk to the gate. A groom leads them in, one at a time, and they stand there with the riders up. None are skittish; all simply go in and stand. After a few minutes the gates open. The babies walk out onto the track. Ahead of them, the expanse of soft dirt, harrowed and raked as smooth as virgin land, lies reddish in the morning sun. The track runs straight and then curves away around the infield, ringed with tall pines and centered on one short, vast tree in the infield. The babies walk a few yards on the track, and stop, and go back to their stables. It's not much of a walk, but it is something. They have begun.

We are staying at the Green Boundary Club on Border Road in Aiken. It is a country inn, comfortable, clean,

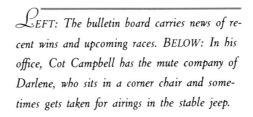

LEFT: The bulletin board carries news of recent wins and upcoming races. BELOW: In his office, Cot Campbell has the mute company of Darlene, who sits in a corner chair and sometimes gets taken for airings in the stable jeep.

OPPOSITE: The Dogwood stable office is a vintage Victorian.

genteel, and idiosyncratic. Some rooms have two baths. Aiken itself is redolent of a time when the Whitneys and the Mellons came down to winter their horses here and to create an equine-based society deep in the Carolinas. Along Whiskey Road the houses are wide and white, with large lawns and deep verandas. The pines and the eucalyptus trees whisper softly of old money. The main street is wide and clean. There is a Court Tennis club in town, one of only a few in this country. It is indoors, the rackets are long-handled, and the tennis balls are heavy. All shots are in play, including some off the walls and angles (as in racquetball). We try a few strokes on the court, empty in the late morning. Joan remains haughtily above the contest. Our friend Helen Brann has asked me not to speak of it. I, a natural athlete, avoid serious injury.

Like a lot of small places, Aiken entertains often at home. Drinks, dinner, and talk of horses. Japanese lanterns seemed to float in the green darkness of the Campbells' backyard. An elderly black man in a white jacket moved softly about the living room serving drinks, taking orders for more. Joan and I were there. She looked beautiful. I wore a tie. There were some stuffed mushrooms, and little turnovers that contained cheese; and there was bourbon on ice, and with water, and foamed with soda from a siphon. And then there was dinner. A Southern dinner, a dinner to dazzle the palate and quicken the heartbeat of any omnivorous city kid who happened by. Show the Yankees a little bit about cooking. There was pork barbecue, Carolina-style, shredded and simmered in the barbecue sauce until sauce and meat were nearly one. There were barbecued beans and there was cole-slaw, there were biscuits and there was something that

The stable office porch offers a good view of the barns.

appeared to be mostly gravy, and there was beer to soothe everything along. I ate rather a lot of everything, fearing at any moment that an undercover man from the *Tufts Nutrition Letter* would appear through the patio door and clap the cuffs on me.

"We can never eat at Lutèce again," Joan whispered to me.

"Don't tell," I said.

$\mathcal{D}$inner at the Campbells'.

The dinner did not end with sweet potato pie; but life is imperfect, and adults accept it. Later, after the evening ended, Joan and I walked a little of the barbecue off along Border Road. Aiken does not stay up late. There was no one else on Border Road, occasionally a car going slowly, as things do in Aiken. Otherwise there was only us, and the occasional night-bird sound among the trees along the roadway, and very far above, the stars. We held hands. We didn't talk.

Ah, wilderness!

MIAMI:
GULFSTREAM

There are two major tracks in Miami: Gulfstream and Hialeah. Hialeah is the one with the flamingos. This afternoon we are at Gulfstream, in Cot's box in the Turf Club. There are very few bad seats at the track. What makes a good seat has much to do with the status attached to it. Coats and ties are required in the Turf Club. Since I have an eighteen-inch neck, my tie tends to look like the hawser from a toy boat. Joan wears a straw hat. Not the kind Rita Hayworth used to wear; the kind Gilbert Roland used to wear. I expect her to break out a small thin black cigar and say, *Ai, chihuahua.*

She doesn't.

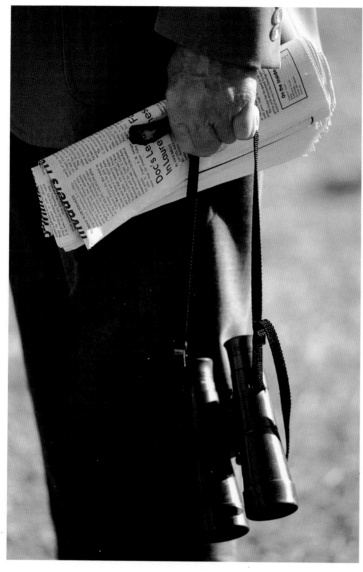

In the walking ring, this jockey is holding a pot of petunias.

Orfano is going to run. He's been hurt and recuperating, and now he's healthy but overweight, and they are going to run him simply for the experience, to ease him back into racing today. No one expects him to win. We each have a program. Helen has a racing form. Helen knows about betting and racing. She can and does play

The walking ring has the air of a Florida garden party.

triples and exactas, she talks easily of boxing several bets, and in general speaks at the track a language as arcane as the theory of time-space continuum. Joan and I ask her to place a bet for us; we don't know how.

ABOVE: Condominiums almost over-shadow the horses running down the back-stretch. RIGHT: The call to the post—the horses are on the track . . .

"Trifecta?" she says.

"Number three to win," I say.

Helen nods. That would be a difficult bet. She checks her form again, makes some notes on her betting plans, takes my fifty-dollar bill, and heads off to the windows. There is a lake in the infield, with a miniature paddle wheeler cruising about in it. Across the bay, the high-rise condominiums are a backdrop to the track. We are some distance from Saratoga. The clubhouse is nearly full, but not crowded. It's a good-looking crowd, well dressed, a lot of people from two places here. The men are in jackets. Their ties look good; none resembles the hawser on a toy boat. I am consoled that I have a good-looking wife. Helen comes back from betting. One advantage of the Turf Club—the windows are not so crowded. She gives me my ticket. We settle back to look at the proceedings.

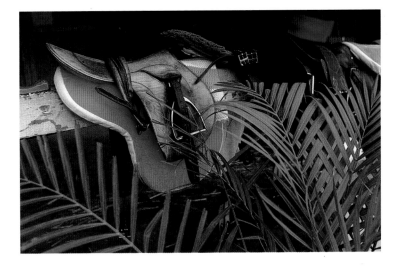

One of the things one learns at the track is that much time is spent when the horses aren't running. Like baseball, there's a lot of down time, and like baseball there is time to talk about the sport, and like baseball the talk is nearly always about the same things: great names from the past. Statistics are trotted out, but instead of batting

average and RBI, it's winnings. I find it interesting as I listen. It is always money. There is some talk of how fast a horse ran; a lot of talk about how much he won. That is the throbbing heart and vital soul of racing— money. Racing is funded by parimutuel betting, which is why there is so much time between races to talk of money. There has to be time for anyone who wants to get his money down. Not many go to watch them run. It would be like playing poker for matchsticks. As Fast Eddie Felson once remarked, money won is twice as sweet as money earned.

The first race is formed, the horses are in the starting gate, they're off. Number three wins. Helen's several horses do not win, or finish in the way they were sup-

They approach the gate.

posed to in order for her to win. I go to the window, emboldened by victory, and collect my winnings. After one race, Joan and I are three hundred dollars ahead. Everyone is impressed.

"How did you pick him?" Helen says.

"Bet the jockey," I say cryptically. Everyone nods appreciatively as if to say, He looks like some kind of city-bred lout with a funny necktie, but he's got a real feel for the sport.

In truth, I had bet the jockey. Angel Cordero. I'd seen him interviewed once on television, a tiny man with the hands and forearms of a stone mason. He was the only creature, human or animal, that I had ever heard of in the first race.

Joan and I win again in the second race. We bet a horse called Larrupin' Lou, because we like the name. It pays four to one. We are up five hundred dollars. Helen has bet a combination that sounds somewhat like the formula for measuring the movement of subatomic particles. She loses again. The two innocents, who wouldn't know *early foot* from *strong finish*, are winning; the veteran and savvy horse player is not. The veteran and savvy horse player finds this less amusing than I do. Joan gives me one of

Jockey Jean-Luc Samyn,
wearing the Dogwood silks,
gets his prerace instructions
from trainer Howie Tesher

her looks, the one that says, *Why not be a little quieter?*
But I am swollen with hubris.

"I think I'll bet that cute black horsie in the third race,"
I say.

My companions grit their teeth.

"On the nose," I say, trying out my racetrack lingo.
"I'm going to drop a C-note on his nose."

Everyone is intent on watching the horses as they circle the track, heading for the starting gate. I swagger
up, drop a hundred dollars on the cute black horsie to

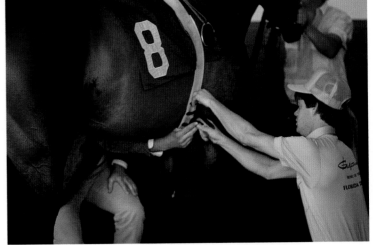

. . . while Orfano gets his
girth fastened in the saddling
stall.

114

RIGHT: Orfano warming up. BELOW: In the box at Gulfstream—Cot Campbell, Helen Brann and Joan.

win, and walk back to my box in the Turf Club, erect, confident, unembarrassed by my necktie. I have the bearing of a man playing on their money.

The cute black horsie finishes forty lengths out. He is so far behind, he is almost in the next race. Apparently no one else in my box has bet him. They all seem very cheery in my box.

Orfano runs in the next race. Even out of loyalty we don't bet. Even on the track, decked out in saddle and

The start.

silks and jockey, Orfano looks a little plump. He finishes next to last. As expected.

Humbled by the betrayal of the cute black horsie, I am trying to learn. I glance at the racing form, read the program, consider the weights, and consult others around me. I also take in the crowd a little. In the next box is a beautiful woman with blue-black hair and pale skin. She wears the kind of straw hat that Rita Hayworth did wear—white, with a wide brim and a flowered band. She has a soft white dress, as well, which swirls about her and sets off the ivory tone of her skin. She speaks Spanish to her companion. Behind us is a famous trainer, quite old now, very elegant in a yellow shirt and gold collar pin. The famous trainer is from Argentina. Outside the Turf Club restaurant I run into Dick Francis, the writer. A former British jockey and steeplechase rider, he now lives in Florida and sells more books than I do. I hate that.

The betting windows range across the back of the Turf Club. There are television monitors where one can watch the race and still remain close to one's money. There are monitors on which the odds are displayed and updated as they change. The betting windows themselves are automated. There is a teller at each, but his, or her, function

Orfano comes back, a little the worse for wear.

is ever-increasingly that of a computer keyboard operator. Some people take a long time at the window, some are quick. I always like to bet on one horse, to win. It's uncomplicated, and it allows me to concentrate all my rooting energy on one beast, all the way around the track.

In addition to the Turf Club restaurant, with a good view of the track, there is a bar, just past the betting booths. It affords no view of the track, but there are the omnipresent monitors. So one could come here, drink beer, bet on the horses, and watch the races on television. I didn't see many who opted for that choice. I toyed with it; it was such a *city* thing to do.

But I didn't.

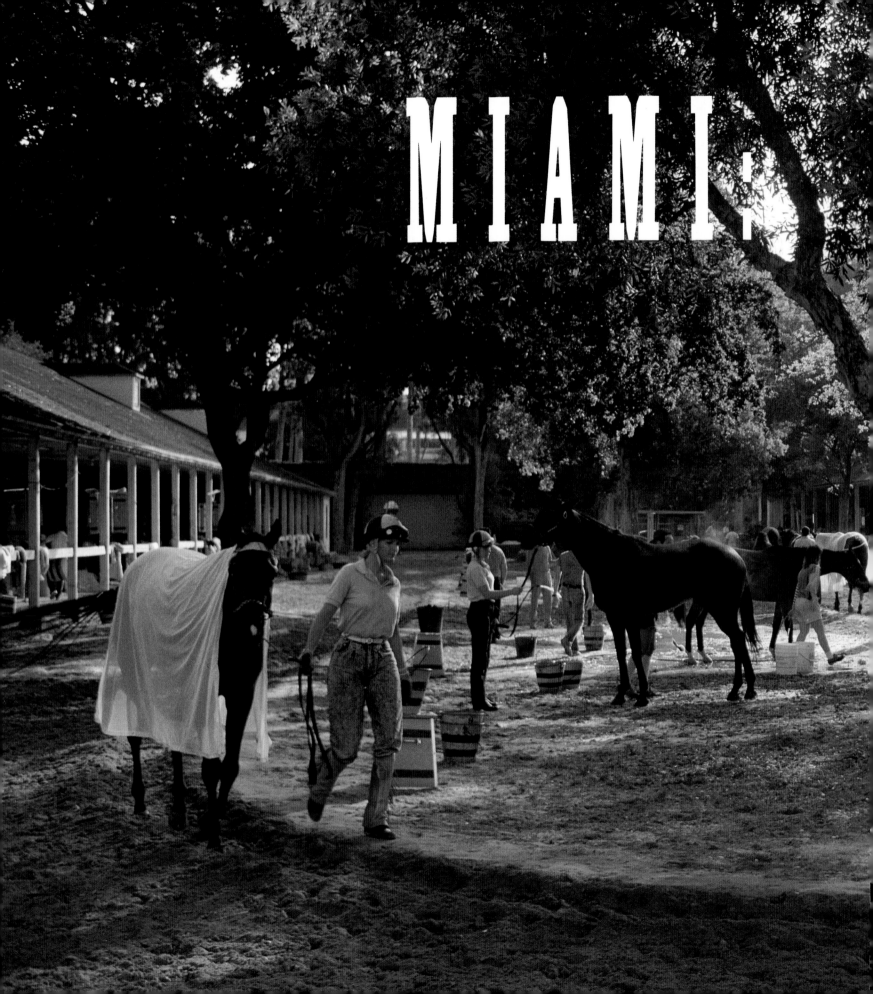

MIAMI:

HIALEAH

Riding a set of horses from the barn to the track at Hialeah.

Hialeah is in the western part of Miami, north of the airport. It is in, I am told, a less desirable part of Miami. This was a little puzzling to Joan and me, because as far as we could tell, all of Miami was the less desirable part.

We are staying on Miami Beach, in one of those old, legendary, beachfront art deco resort hotels where insurance men from Yonkers come for sales conferences and get to join the president's circle or the academy of honor by selling unseemly amounts of life insurance, often to relatives. Such hotels are careful to see that no food-phobic insurance salesperson or his or her family should ever have to eat something they have not eaten often at home in Yonkers. The food is overcooked, high in saturated fat, low in fiber, bland, unattractive to the eye, and meager. Meager is the good news.

From our hotel it's straight west across the bay over the Kennedy Causeway. We go in the morning. They aren't racing at Hialeah; we are going to look at the racetrack. If Gulfstream is Yin, Hialeah is Yang. Gulfstream is new-looking, smooth of contour, slick of facing, with the high-rise condos. It is the Miami recently created—efficient, accommodating, and, sadly, a little soulless. Hialeah is old and Spanish-looking. The walls are stucco; there are flowers everywhere. There are flamingos living in a lake

Cot Campbell watches his horses work out.

in the infield. Hialeah is old Miami; there's a hint of shabbiness lurking behind the bougainvillea. It speaks of money and fun and class and, maybe, of better times.

We are there having breakfast and listening to a good-looking woman on a peaceable gelding talk about horse racing through a microphone to a bunch of kids and a few adult tourists gathered near her at the finish line. Behind her, the flamingos dash around on the ground and occasionally glide into the air for short distances. I am drinking coffee, watching the birds, as the woman explains about bloodlines. As I watch, a hawk floats in from the southeast and turns lazy circles over the flamingos. They don't like it. They rush about. The hawk is not big enough to do them any harm, but they don't seem to know that. Perhaps flamingos are not terribly smart. After teasing the flamingos awhile, the hawk turns and heads elsewhere. Maybe Gulfstream. The woman on the horse talks on. It is interesting, but I know most of it. I sip coffee and feel the Florida sun on my face. I admire the way the woman's riding clothes fit her. Joan notices this.

"I'm studying the horse," I said.

Joan smiles at me, which is always something to see.

"Of course you are," she said. "Very alert of you."

When the woman finishes, we stroll about the nearly empty track. It is odd, and somehow exciting, to be alone in the echoing emptiness of a normally busy place. Everything about this track—the betting windows, the high-ceilinged white-tile washroom, the dull gleam of polished wood—whispers of the sport of kings, in a way that few tracks any longer do. We walk through the courtyard

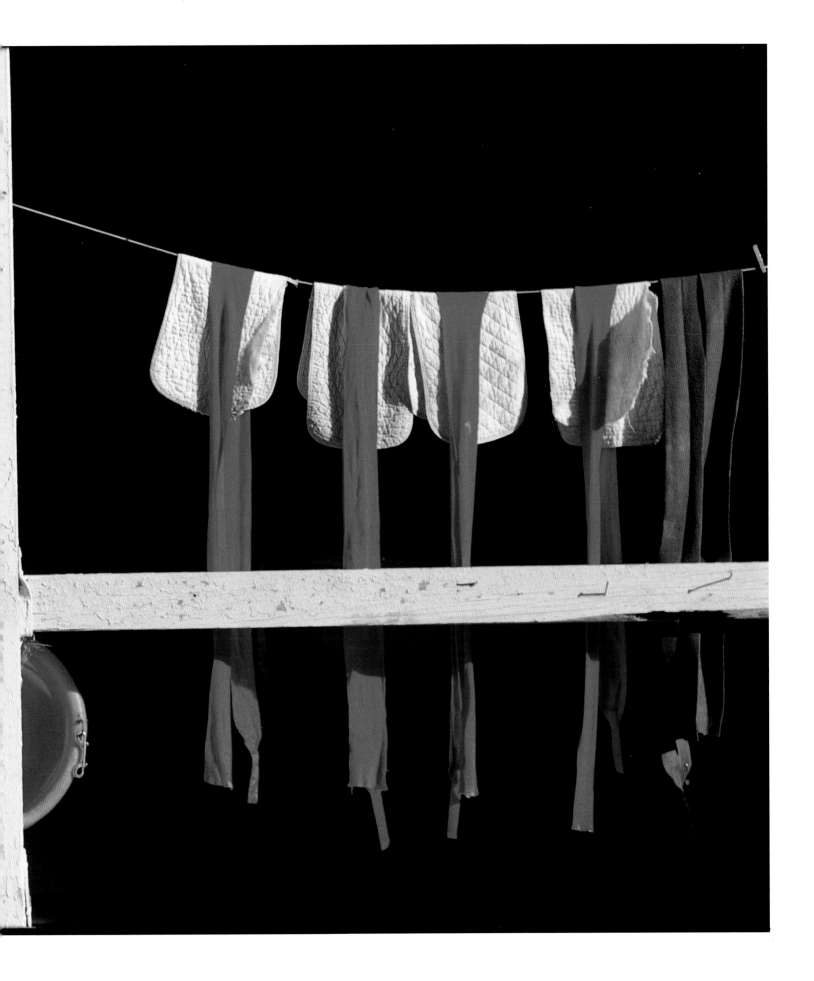

and to the backside, where the horses are. Even though they're not running, they're stabled here. Orfano, fresh from not being last at Gulfstream, is led out. His brown coat gleams like the soft rubbed wood in the clubhouse. He is still a little fat, the musculature in his shoulders a little muted by it, his haunches a little higher by it. A fat racehorse is by no means a porker. But every extra ounce must be lugged around the track, and contributes nothing to the effort.

Weight is a matter of continuous attention: the horses' weight, the jockeys' weight. And as both get older, the weight tends to become more and more problematic. The horse can retire to stud. For the jockey it's career-threatening. He diets, he steams, he runs, he may take unsafer measures, and every day the scale is there, the icon of his final dissolution. At 111, he's everybody's all-American. At 120, he's an exercise boy. In no other endeavor, not boxing, not crew, do strength and weight fight such a continuous war. Jockeys need to be strong, they need to be small. They also need to be tough. They need to be willing—in fact, eager—to jam this half-ton animal into a moment of daylight along the rail, where jostling is common and falls occur and death is not unheard of.

One of the Dogwood horses has some company.

Jockeys are marvelous athletes, like the horses; and the weight hangs over them from their first apprentice ride until the last time they climb down and walk off the track.

Orfano submits to some patting. Cot and the trainer talk a bit about his further training. Everyone is confident that his injury is healed and his weight will soon be where it should be . . . if he stays away from Joe's.

Joe's Stone Crabs is at the bottom of Miami Beach. A pleasant, ordinary-looking restaurant where one can eat stone crab and hash-brown potatoes and creamed spinach and Key lime pie that is unequaled anywhere on the planet. We ate there with the Campbells. We over-

Cot is pleased with his colt's progress.

ordered and ate everything. Even Joan ate a lot. I managed to get through the evening without making a scene over the last crab claw. Joan was proud of me.

Later we drove the rental car up Collins Avenue past rows of hotels that looked vaguely like Iraqi bus stations.

"This sporting life ain't bad," I said.

"I fear if we lived it too long we'd die early," Joan said.

"But happy," I said.

"We're that anyway," she said.

It was nearly nine-thirty in the evening. No one was about along the beach. From the art deco windows in the rococo hotels, the bluish glow of television sets spilled into the soft subtropic light. Above us there was a half-moon.

"Remember the song 'Moon over Miami'?" I said.

"Yes," Joan said.

"Want me to sing a couple of choruses?" I said.

Catching up on the Racing Form *in the tack room.*

"No," Joan said.

"That's just because you're not a romantic," I said.

"No," Joan said. "It's because I am."

AIKEN: THE TRIALS

It is time for the babies to run. The yearlings bought last year at Saratoga and Keeneland auctions are here, in Aiken, in spring, ready for their first race. The Aiken trials are a festival with horses. There is no formal betting, no parimutuel windows at the Aiken training track adjacent to the Dogwood barn. It was here, last November, that the young horses first stood in the gate and stared down the empty track and saw the gate open and walked a few yards without incident. Now the track is still empty, but along the rails, and on the open grassy meadows ringed with tall pines, there are crowds.

Aiken's finest are augmented with auxiliary police for

Elegant picnics are the order of the day.

the Aiken trials. Traffic fills the narrow country roads that lead into the training track. We drive slowly, in a Dogwood vehicle, directed by one of the auxiliary police-men to the reserved area where owners and others of special status may watch the trials and picnic. There is a much larger area, where it is park as park can and the picnics lean more toward beer than wine and the air is resonant with the output of oversize portable radios.

$\mathcal{H}$ats and parasols offer some protection from the Carolina sun.

I'm watching the Gatsby party through my shades, while the younger set gets involved in a different kind of horse race.

ABOVE: On the rail is Susan Keenan (RIGHT), one of Summer Squall's owners.

It is March, and in South Carolina it is hot. We in the reserved area are wearing jackets and ties. In the unreserved area, people frolic shirtless among the pickup trucks. Dogwood is entering a colt named Summer Squall, for whom there is much hope. Everyone agrees this is just the way to introduce the colt to competition. Doesn't matter if he wins. Doesn't matter what his time is. Just want to get his feet wet. It all makes perfect sense. The same things are said in spring training every year. I don't believe it then, either.

At the far end of the reserved area there are people having a Gatsby party. Guests are wearing gossamer white gowns like Daisy Buchanan, and white suits with straw hats like Nick Carraway. There is a sky-blue parasol. There is a good-looking blond woman in a flowered dress and another in a rainbow-striped straw with a big brim and flowers at the back of the band. The food may be classified as picnic in that it is served outdoors, but it is hardly commonplace. Anne Campbell serves us thin slices of rare roast tenderloin of beef. There is salad. There are croissants and Linzer tortes. There is a bottle of Chablis, straw-colored in the bright spring sunlight.

Across the track, people are watching from the infield,

not picnicking, just leaning on the inside rail, or sitting

on folding chairs under the one squat wide tree, so striking

that it seems contrived. It is near ninety as post tim

approaches. Most men have shed their coats and ties.

Along the rail there is no shade, and many in the crowd

have drifted back into the shade of the tall pines near

the tree line. At one of the parties a gentleman has set

up a small racetrack machine, in which toy horses spin

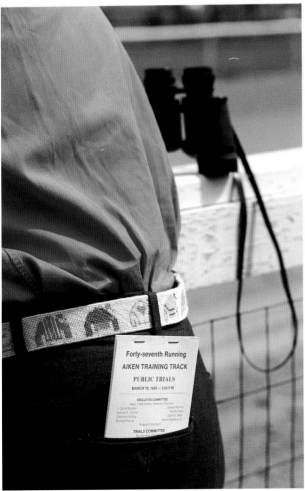

around a green felt track and bets can be placed. Helen bets and wins. It is the only bet we shall place today. I am told people bet informally among each other, but I don't see any betting.

Joan and I take a walk before the races start. We leave the reserved enclave and plunge into the unreserved section. There is music. There are Frisbees. There are black Labrador dogs with red kerchiefs instead of collars. There are more pickup trucks here, and more vans. The oversize blast boxes play loud, indecipherable music, and there are hot dogs grilling over portable burners. The sound of beer cans popping, the smell of hops. Small children wearing plastic-mesh baseball caps adjusted down to the smallest size.

*Julie and Summer Squall
jog down to the start.*

*Julie Stewart, Summer
Squall's exercise rider, has
her first racing ride today.*

We walked back to the paddock, somewhat informally created by roping off an area between the reserved and unreserved sections. Summer Squall will be ridden by a young woman listed in the program as J. Stewart. She is an exercise rider, and this is her first racing ride. In her Dogwood green and yellow, she seems calm enough as Ron Stevens talks with her. The horses are edgy; one rears and snorts. I am the only one who seems to notice. The riders are up, the horses led out to the starting gate. We take our place at the rail. Behind us, on the hood of Cot's Jaguar, the remnants of lunch linger alluringly. Shame to waste that tenderloin. Very lean. May as well have a couple. Joan has her straw hat tilted forward, shading her eyes.

All along the rail, on both sides, the crowd quiets. The boom boxes from the unreserved area are silenced. The colt that was skittish in the paddock is skittish at the gate, but finally he's in. They're all in. There's a pause, as always. And then they're off and here they come. This is a sprint, a quarter mile, straight down the track, finishing just past us. No turns, no time to fight for position. There is not much strategy available in a quarter of a mile. These are full-grown animals. They don't look like

At the finish, Summer Squall is third, barely beaten for second place.

babies; nearly two years old, they seem like any of the horses we have seen . . . until now. Now they are babies. They run like babies. Legs flailing, eyes wide, heads outstretched, they come without restraint, helter-skelter down the track, with a look of wild-eyed bewilderment—*What in hell am I doing here?*—and a posture of total abandonment—*Look at me run!* There is exuberance in the race, the babies run with a kind of untrained ecstasy, and it is over, almost at once. A gray colt with a look

of perfect madness finishes first, just ahead of Summer
Squall.

No one expresses any sorrow that Summer Squall didn't
win. Everyone is pleased with his time, with his track sense,
with his racing style. He's going to be a good one. He
will go on, less than three months later, to win the Kentucky Budweiser Breeder's Cup. But now, on a hot day

*Congratulations are due
anyway—they had a good
trip.*

in Aiken in March, he has made his first wild dash for the finish, and people have cheered him and his career has begun.

There are other races. There is an exhibition of carriage driving, and later in the day, sated with rare tenderloin and hammered by a persistent sun, we go back to the inn for a nap. Later we will dine with the Campbells' daughter Leila and her husband, Lawson Glenn. But the day centers on that frantic dash of untutored horses in the middle of a picnic. It is a lovely image.

ABOVE: Jack Seabrook's team of grays gives an exhibition of carriage driving. RIGHT: A post-race party keeps the celebration going.

EPILOGUE

I t is a perfect *August day. Seventy six degrees, sunny. Summer Squall is running in the Hopeful Stakes, and we are in Saratoga to watch* him. Back where we began a year ago, Joan still looks clubhouse. I still look (albeit dashingly) backstretch, and Summer Squall, whom we saw as a splay-footed wild-eyed yearling taking second in the Aiken trials, is now the pre-eminent two-year-old in the country.

The Hopeful is the launching pad for great horses. Citation won the Hopeful, so did Man O'War and Secretariat and Seattle Slew. For Cot and Anne Campbell this is the supreme adventure in twenty-five years of racing. It is also our thirty-third wedding anniversary. The excitement is palpable.

153

The Hopeful is the eighth race—as always, the feature race. The Campbells will sit tensely through seven others. In a display of ferocious self-control, they are cheery, charming, funny. Around them are perhaps a dozen of Summer Squall's forty owners, nearly as tense as the Campbells and showing it more. We are in the clubhouse. I was edgy coming in and stayed close to Joan, but no one told me to go to the backstretch, and once past the usher I was able to loosen my tie. The fifth race is underway when we arrive. We sit with Helen, and talk of business a bit. This book is not our only enterprise. I brag about my sons, go out for a Häagen-Dazs fruit bar (pineapple), mull over the program. No one bets. Everyone is too nervous. I am not nervous, I hope things go well, I like the Campbells; but for Joan and for me, it is rather like being observers at a war among other coun-

On Hopeful Day, assistant trainer Jim Pinkston checks the bandages that will help protect Summer Squall from injury.

They make the long walk from the barn to the track.

Summer Squall's groom, Willie Woods, looks more nervous than his horse as they enter the paddock.

*C*ot (LEFT), jockey Pat Day
(CENTER), and trainer Neil Howard
(RIGHT) show the tension as they wait for
their horse.

tries. Crucial things are happening, but they aren't happening to us.

The seventh race unfolds. No one much notices. Then it is time for the eighth. We trail Cot and Anne down to the paddock, where Summer Squall and the others are led out, looked at, walked around. Trainer Neil Howard is there. Pat Day, the elfin jockey, comes to talk with Cot. He weighs approximately half what I weigh. His hands are bigger than mine and look as if he borrowed them from a stone mason. Day seems perfectly calm. He does this, after all, every day. He has done this already six times today. But not on this horse, in this race, with the future on the line, on our wedding anniver-

sary. I decide not to mention the anniversary. There's enough pressure already. Joan compliments me on my sensitivity.

If Pat Day seems calm, Summer Squall is practically bucolic. He ambles about the paddock with his groom, a young black man in a baseball cap, named Willie Woods. Willie's head is close to his, Willie murmurs things to him. Summer Squall says nothing, but he seems in agree-

ment. Under the green trees, with the crowd pressed against the white fence and the smell of sausages frying in the distance, Summer Squall is as serene as if Willie were going to stroll him to the creek. Howard saddles him, careful with the blanket, careful with the cinch, then Day is up, and the blue-uniformed track police are making way for the horses as they head through a corridor of onlookers toward the track. We follow and then hurry to the clubhouse as the horses veer off onto the track itself.

"Is there time for another Häagen-Dazs fruit bar?" Joan says.

"It's our anniversary," I say.

We stop at the vendor. Joan gets lemon-lime, I opt again for pineapple. We lap our fruit bars as we edge through the crowd toward our box.

"Do I know how to show you a good time," I say, "or what?"

Joan smiles, the way Mona Lisa does, and says nothing. Over the speaker system the track announcer says, "And they're off."

Yikes!

Joan and I stop edging and begin pushing through the

Summer Squall bursts through the pack . . .

. . . opens a daylight lead . . .

crowd. It's one of the few things I'm good at, and what Joan lacks in bulk she makes up in vigor. In a moment we are in view of the race as they go into the first turn. Summer Squall is running easily, Pat Day hand-riding him (no whip), waiting. They string out a little along the backstretch and then come around the last turn and into the stretch. Summer Squall looks to be in fifth place, behind four leaders bunched, with Adjudicating on the rail and Sir Richard Lewis swinging wide on the outside. *Fifth. Entering the stretch.* Carson City is on Adjudicat-

. . . and crosses the wire well in front.

ing's right shoulder and Bite the Bullet has drifted a little wider toward Sir Richard Lewis. Suddenly, in the upper stretch, there is a sliver of daylight between Bite the Bullet and Carson City. Pat Day sticks Summer Squall's nose into that sliver just as it begins to close. From where I stand on the plaza behind the clubhouse boxes, with my pineapple fruit bar melting unattended in my hand, it looks as if jockey Craig Perret turns Bite the Bullet in toward the rail to close out Summer Squall. They bump, Summer Squall staggers, bumps Carson City on his left, and

should be dropping back and losing. He doesn't. He keeps his head wedged in the space and then bulls his shoulders in, squirming, swinging his head, his ears back flat, his neck out straight. He churns into the hole jostling Bite the Bullet on his outside, and Carson City on his inside, keeping his feet, keeping his twenty-foot stride, with Pat Day crouched over his neck, both of them buffeted by more than a ton of full-gallop horse, and then Summer Squall is through, his feet under him, and in the lead.

"Hugh McEllenny," I say. Out loud. To nobody.

Summer Squall opens the lead with a furlong left and crosses the finish line looking as if he could have run to Albany. Sir Richard Lewis second, Eternal Flight third.

"My God," Joan says.

We head for the Campbells' box, full of congratula-

*W*illie Woods leads Summer Squall into the winner's circle.

tions. But the tension hasn't dissipated.

"Cot says there's a problem," Anne Campbell says.

In the infield the tote board announces a steward's inquiry. Summer Squall's number, 4, in its winner position, keeps flashing on and off, indicating that its status is under question. Photographers gather around the Campbells and trainer Neil Howard. Summer Squall is led to the winner's circle, unsaddled, walked away by Willie, their heads close, as calm as he had been in the paddock. The cameras grind away, the power drives making their little whir. The photographers will throw most of the film away. But with their backs to the tote board, facing owner and trainer, they have to keep shooting, waiting for the reaction shot, the one they all want, when the decision becomes official.

"And if they decide it's a foul, Summer Squall loses?" Joan says.

"Un huh."

On the tote board number 4 keeps flashing.

"And everyone will have to turn around and leave the winner's circle and walk back into the stands?"

"Un huh."

"That's barbaric," Joan says.

"Yes."

We stand watching the tote board, where 4 flashes in a slow pulse, too slow, so that each flash seems to be the last and false hopes keep rising only to be dashed. The water trucks that sprinkle the track after each race come slowly by. The track police move us out of harm's way. And still the inquiry goes on. And still number 4

𝒩*ow, an agonizing wait, watching the tote board to see if Summer Squall will be disqualified.*

keeps flashing; for eighteen minutes at too slow a pulse. Then it stops and the 4 remains. And the word *Official* replaces *Inquiry* and the owners erupt, including Cot, who had, until now stood impassively watching the tote board, his binoculars characteristically slung over his shoulder.

Later we have dinner with him.

"What did you do," Joan asks, "after the decision, and the champagne in the directors' room? On the greatest triumph of your life."

It's official! He's won it.

A happy group holds the
trophy for the winner of the
Hopeful Stakes.

He paused a moment while the waitress passed out a platter of sliced tomatoes and the tinny piano in the bar played "Sweet Rosie O'Grady," and he looked at his wife.

"We went to see the horse," he said. "At a time like that the best thing to do is to go and look at the horse."

*M*uch later, alone at the romantic Ramada Inn in Saratoga, Joan and I exchanged anniversary gifts.

"You know what I like?" she said. "I like the way, when Cot was headed for the winner's circle and Anne was three or four people behind him, in the crowd? I like how he stopped and looked for her. He wasn't going out there without her."

Summer Squall has a quiet victory celebration . . .

I nodded.

"What was that you said about Hugh McEllsomething?" Joan said.

"McEllenny," I said, "Hugh McEllenny."

"Why'd you say that?"

I shook my head.

"Too much to explain," I said.

Joan's disinterest in football legends is exceeded only by her affection for me. She smiled.

"Some horse," she said.

Outside, the pleasant upstate town was still. No cars went past on Route 9, no students in stylish disarray trucking down from Skidmore. Nothing was open, only street lights gave color to the green of lawn and trees. A mile away Summer Squall was sleeping standing up the way horses do, dreaming maybe long equine dreams; not knowing that his life had changed entirely today when he had busted through the moment of daylight the way Hugh McEllenny used to; not even thinking about how nothing after this would ever be the same; dreaming, if horses dream at all, of oats, maybe, or mares, or running fast; entirely unaware of what he had carried with him this day. But the people knew. The Campbells most of all.

"Some horse," I said.

. . . as Cot and Anne Campbell watch.

Afterword

Fourteen months after his wide-eyed dash down the quarter-mile stretch in the Aiken trials, Summer Squall was at Churchill Downs at the clubhouse turn, head to head with a big muscular colt named Unbridled. The rest of the field was behind them. We who knew him waited for him to shift into that other gear. The crowd roared. Summer Squall cocked his ears for a moment, eased back for a moment, and didn't shift. He finished second to Unbridled in the Kentucky Derby. And we all waited with odd knots in our stomachs for the Preakness and redemption.

When it came, it came as it should have. Unbridled on the last turn swung outside the front runner, Fight-

JERRY FRUTKOFF

174

ing Notion, and headed home as he had in the Derby. Summer Squall stayed inside, and when Fighting Notion drifted a little off the rail on the turn, Pat Day put Summer Squall's nose into the daylight. Summer Squall passed Fighting Notion on the inside as Unbridled went past him on the outside. For maybe two lengths they hung there like that.

"Not twice," Joan said.

The gear clicked in, as it always had, except once. Challenged on his right as he had been at the Derby, Summer Squall exploded. He ran the last three-sixteenths of a mile in 18 seconds, something even Secretariat had never done, to win the Preakness.

"You were right," I said.

"What?" Joan said.

"Not twice," I said.

A NOTE ON THIS BOOK

This edition of A Year at the Races *was set in Cloister and Liberty by International Graphic Services of Edison, New Jersey. Design was by Amy Hill with Liney Li. The display type was set in photographically condensed Grecian Bold by Ultratypographic Services, New York, New York. The book was printed on 86# gloss coated paper and has a Smythe sewn binding. Toppan International Group, of Tokyo, Japan, did color separations and printed and bound the book.*